To Abi and Ruby, our bright stars,
always in our dreams xxx
S.S.

For Princess Milly, your world is a daydream!
And for Ali, my very own bright star.
C.C.

First published in Great Britain 2017 by Egmont UK Limited
This edition published 2018 by Dean,
an imprint of Egmont UK Limited,
The Yellow Building, 1 Nicholas Road, London, W11 4AN
www.egmont.co.uk

Text copyright © Suzanne Smith 2017
Illustrations copyright © Charlotte Cooke 2017
The moral rights of the author and illustrator have been asserted.

ISBN 978 0 6035 7581 5
70182/003
Printed in Malaysia

A CIP catalogue record for this title is available from the British Library.

The Littlest Dreamer
A BEDTIME JOURNEY

by Suzanne Smith

Illustrated by Charlotte Cooke

DEAN

Little one, little one, eyes closed up tight,
What do you **dream** as you sleep through the night?

What will you **see**?
What will you **play**?
Will you tell me your dreams
when the night becomes day?

Little one, little one, looking at you,
I wonder if all of your dreams will come true.

Do you wish for a marvellous **sky pony** ride
To see wondrous places that stretch far and wide?

Would you **ride up a rainbow** and look down below,
Gazing on meadows where sweet flowers grow?

Do you wonder if **fairies** might sing a sweet tune
As they **dance** in the light of the glowing full moon?

Do they **flutter** and **fly** with their sparkling wings
Through a garden of magical toadstool rings?

Do you wish for a ride on a bright dragonfly,
To go chasing fireflies ever so high?

Would you **dart in and out**
of the moon-dappled leaves,

Holding on tight as you
zoom through the trees?

Do you wonder if, late on a midsummer's night,
The **animals feast** in the moon's silver light?

Would you join them for cakes with starlight and sprinkles,
Toasting marshmallows on a campfire that twinkles?

Do you wish you'd discover a **sugarplum land?**
Would it have a tall castle, as sweet as it's grand?

Could you try **playing catch** with some juicy gumdrops?
Or **climb** to the top of the huge lollipops?

Do you wonder what game the **mermaids** all play
In their watery world at the end of the day?

Do they **ride** on the **seahorses**, play hunt-the-tail,
Or swim really fast as they **race** a great **whale**?

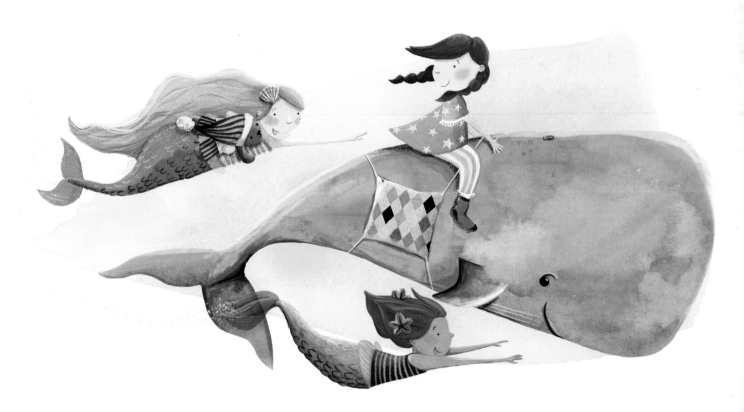

Do you wish you could **ride**
on a **carpet that flies?**
Is it magic that makes it
soar high in the skies?

Would you **dig deep** for riches in some distant land
Till you find treasure buried there under the sand?

Do you wish you were **dressed** in a beautiful gown
And wore a princess's fine golden crown?

Does your heart fill with joy in a splendid marquee
As you dance with a prince at a great jamboree?

Do you wish for the stars that glitter up high
As they sparkle and shine in the inky night sky?

Would they rain down their stardust
to light up your dreams,
As you flew home again
through the magic moonbeams?

Do your wishes and wonders help you to find
Your way back to bed, leaving dreamland behind?

Are they guiding you gently towards the soft light
That shines from your window out into the night?

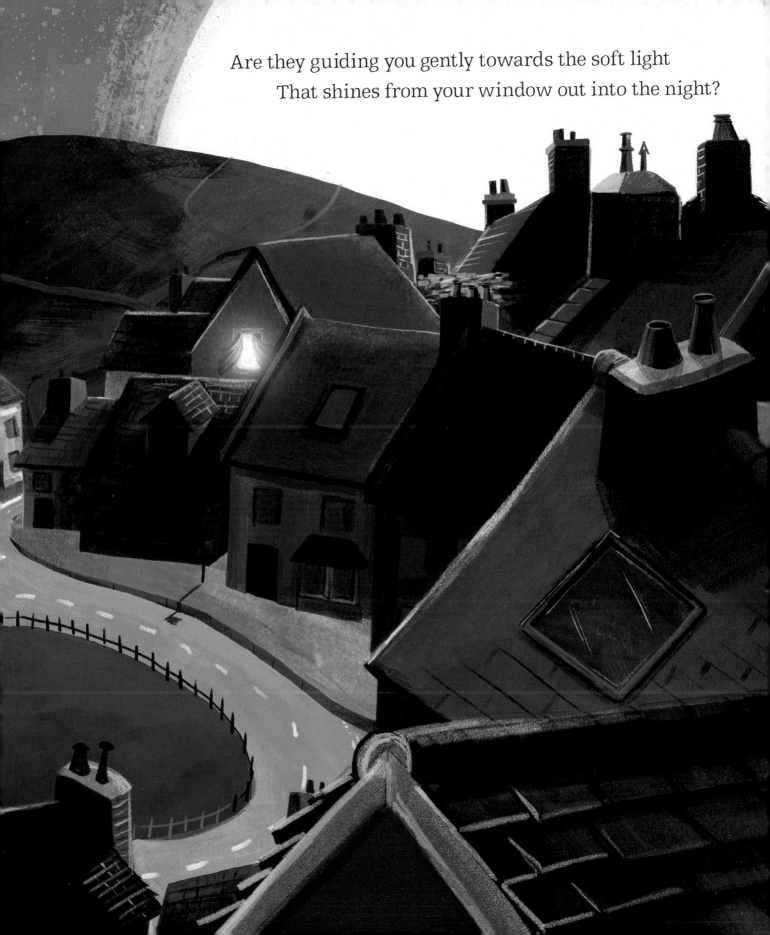

Little one, little one, eyes closed up tight,
What do you **dream** as you sleep through the night?

What will you **see**? What will you **play**?
Will you tell me your dreams when the night becomes day?

Little one, little one, looking at you,
I wonder if all of your dreams will come true.